For Stephen Barr
—G.S.

For Dad and Mom and my "home," Cortland, New York
—L.R.C.

THIS IS A BORZOI BOOK PUBLISHED BY ALFRED A. KNOPF

Text copyright © 2020 by Gideon Sterer
Jacket art and interior illustrations copyright © 2020 by Lucy Ruth Cummins

All rights reserved. Published in the United States by Alfred A. Knopf, an imprint of Random House Children's Books,
a division of Penguin Random House LLC, New York.

Knopf, Borzoi Books, and the colophon are registered trademarks of Penguin Random House LLC.

Visit us on the Web! rhcbooks.com

Educators and librarians, for a variety of teaching tools, visit us at RHTeachersLibrarians.com

Library of Congress Cataloging-in-Publication Data
Names: Sterer, Gideon, author. | Cummins, Lucy Ruth, illustrator.
Title: From Ed's to Ned's / Gideon Sterer ; illustrated by Lucy Ruth Cummins.
Description: First edition. | New York : Alfred A. Knopf, [2020] | Summary: Children whirl, climb, slide, float,
and jump as they go from house to house for playdates.
Identifiers: LCCN 2018020946 | ISBN 978-0-525-64806-2 (trade) | ISBN 978-0-525-64807-9 (lib. bdg.) |
ISBN 978-0-525-64808-6 (ebook)
Subjects: | CYAC: Stories in rhyme. | Play—Fiction.
Classification: LCC PZ8.3.S8283 Fr 2020 | DDC [E]—dc23

The text of this book is set in 40-point Graham.
The illustrations were created using gouache, colored pencil, crayon, brush marker,
charcoal pencil, and chalk and were finished digitally.

MANUFACTURED IN CHINA
June 2020
10 9 8 7 6 5 4 3 2 1

First Edition

FROM ED'S TO NED'S

written by
GIDEON STERER

illustrated by
LUCY RUTH CUMMINS

Alfred A. Knopf  New York

CLIMB to CAL'S

WHIRL to

WILL'S

TRAMPOLINE from TED'S to

JILL'S

TREY'S

SLIDE to SAM'S

SWINGING VINES
from PAUL'S to PAM'S

FLOAT to FRAN'S

DIG to . . .

CANNON-BLAST
from BETH'S

to LUKE'S

JUMP from JIN'S

DIVE to DAN'S

TIGHTROPE-WALK from STEVE'S

to STAN'S

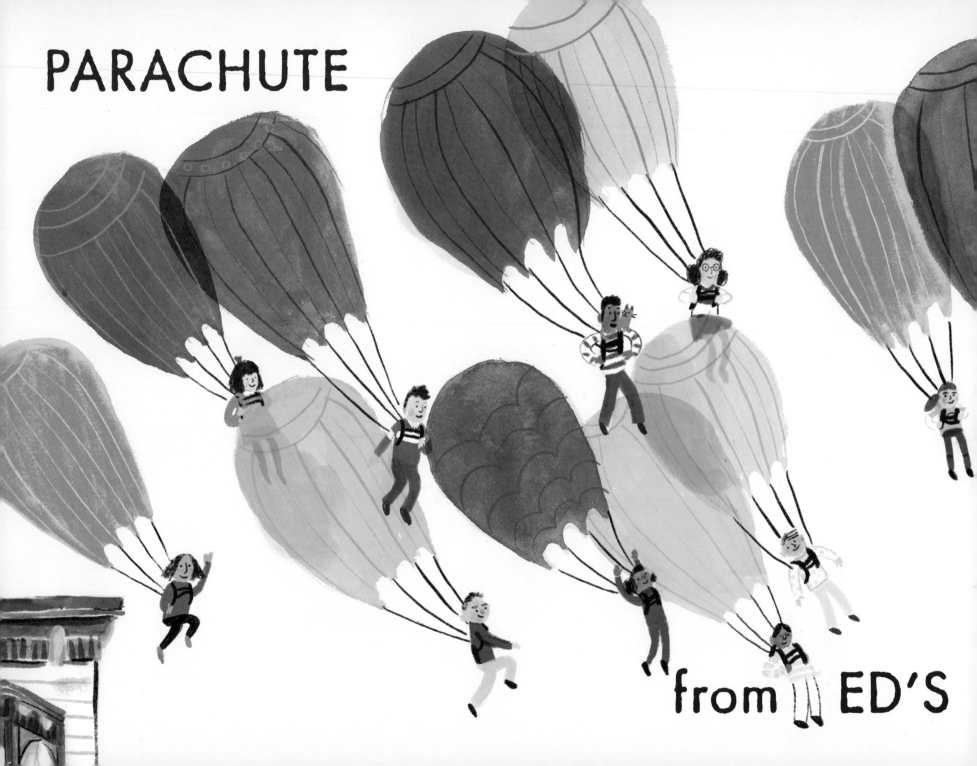

PARACHUTE

from ED'S

to NED'S

Yip-yahoo! What a crew!

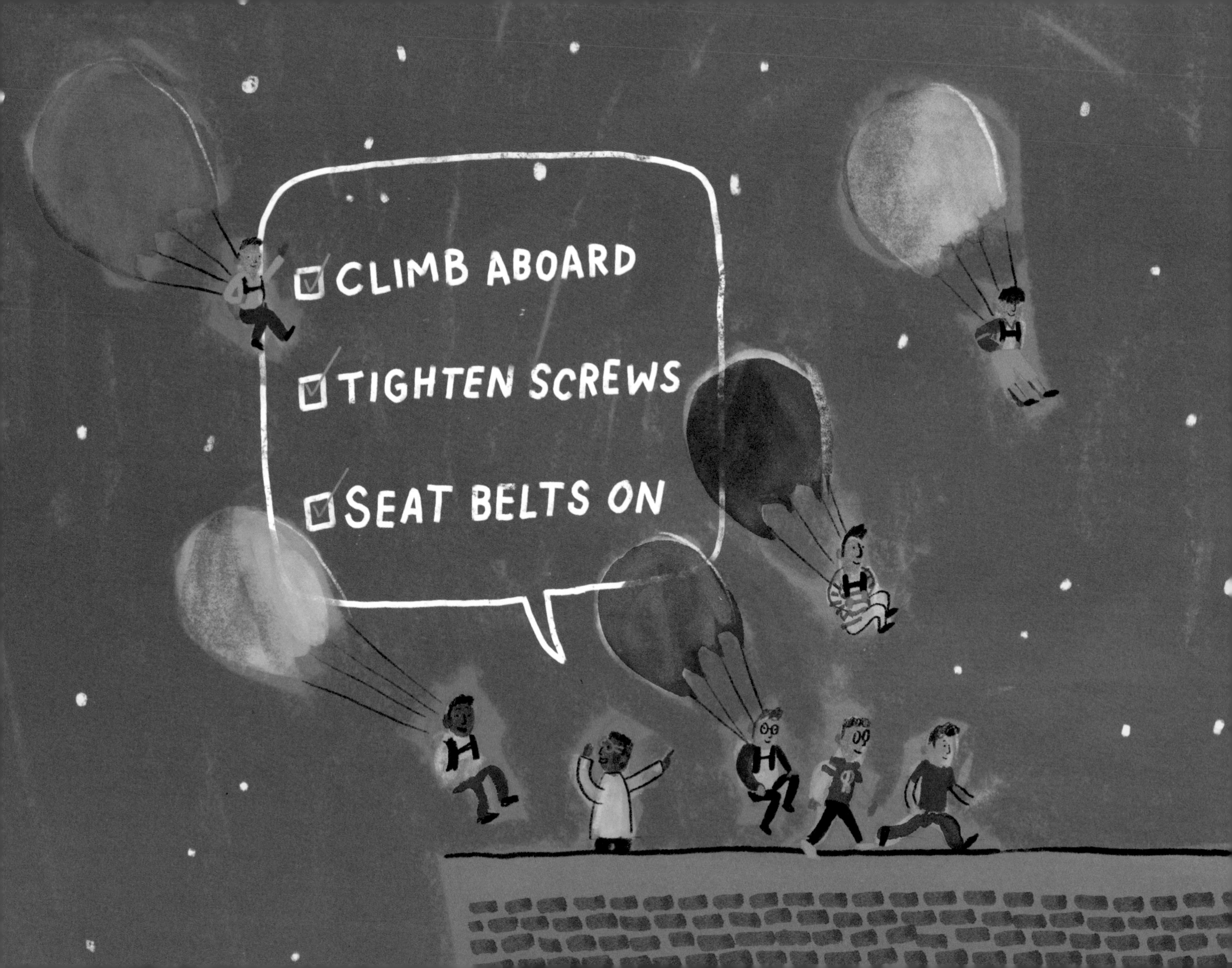
CLIMB ABOARD
TIGHTEN SCREWS
SEAT BELTS ON